2012

Will,

Always reach for the stars!

Sadie Tyler

Herkimer's Big Day

Herkimer the Police Horse Meets a Young Girl Named Sammy

Written by Sandy Tyler

Illustrations by Brian Williams

outskirtspress

Outskirts Press, Inc.
http://www.outskirtspress.com

ISBN: 978-1-4327-9005-9

Library of Congress Control Number: 2012904767

Outskirts Press and the "OP" logo are trademarks belonging to Outskirts Press, Inc.

PRINTED IN THE UNITED STATES OF AMERICA

This book is dedicated to the Quirt n' Crop 4-H Club of Dutchess County, New York.

A special thanks to all the members of the club including our club leader Ann Secor and the Higham's that made the club so special. I would also like to send a special remembrance to another one of the club members, my late sister Jan Haley. Jan and I spent our childhood on horseback riding in parades and shows with the club. The Herkimer character evolved from my experiences in 4-H.

Chapter 1

Sometimes when you think you have everything you have ever dreamed of, your life changes and your whole world is turned upside down. Just such a thing happened to me. Oh, I guess I am getting ahead of myself. My name is Herkimer. I am a police horse. Well, I was a police horse until yesterday when the police department retired me. Just yesterday I was chasing a teenager who had stolen three dozen jelly donuts from Mel's Donut Shop. We chased the thief down Third Street, and

he threw ten donuts at me. I still have the red jelly stains on my coat. We were faster than him, and we caught up to him in record time. Most horses would be afraid of all the lights and sounds of the big city, but not me. I love the excitement of the city.

Today is a sad day for me. I am being loaded onto a horse trailer to go to a horse retirement farm in the country. I have heard that country life is nice with plenty of green pastures to graze on and run through. I would rather be in the big city with all the action and excitement, though.

Chapter 2

I arrived at a beautiful farm with green fields as far as I could see. There were other horses running and playing in the distance. I was put in a field separate from all the other horses. I was lonely all by myself. I spent every day and every night alone while all the other horses were playing and eating together.

I was beginning to think I was going to be lonely forever until this morning. I saw a young girl coming into the barn toward me. She looked as if she had been there before. She started to clean the stalls and throw hay for each of us.

Who is this girl? I thought. She looks really friendly. She is so different than the other kids that hang around the barn. The other children are loud and mean to me. Sammy walked by my stall and then backed up and stopped.

"Well, hello, there. Who are you?" Sammy said. She read my name plate on the door of my stall. "Well, hello, Herkimer. How are you this morning?"

"My name is Sammy P. Nolan," Sammy said. She pet my head and gave me some carrots. I love carrots. "How come you look so sad, Herkimer?" Sammy put a halter and lead rope on me and led me out into the hallway of the barn. She began brushing me and combing my mane.

"Herkimer, what is this sticky stuff all over your coat? You smell just like a jelly donut." Sammy got a wet rag and washed me up. She cleaned all the jelly off my coat and put me back in my stall. "No more jelly for you my friend, just carrots." Sammy smiled and walked away.

I heard the owner of the farm, Fred Ramsey, say, "Hi, Sammy, how are you today?"

"Fine, Fred," Sammy replied. "What's up with the new horse, Herkimer? Where did he come from?"

"Let me tell you all about it over a cold glass of lemonade," Fred said. As Sammy and Fred walked away, Fred looked back at Herkimer and winked. *I wonder what Fred is up to*, Herkimer thought. I watched Fred and Sammy go into the old white farmhouse while the other horses played in the distance.

Chapter 3

The next few days, all I could do was think of Sammy. She is the only kid here at the farm that is nice to me. The other kids call me ugly, and they are right. I look at my reflection in the water trough, and I can see that I am ugly. Who is going to want to ride me? Just as I was feeling really sorry for myself, I saw Sammy again.

"How are you today, Herkimer?" Sammy asked.

Sammy took me out of my stall, brushed me, and put a saddle and bridle on me. Then she led me out of the barn, and we entered a big riding arena.

Sammy lifted herself on to the saddle and asked me to walk. I walked around the arena feeling very proud that Sammy would want to bother with me, the ugly horse. While we rode around the arena, Sammy took me through some obstacles. We jumped over jumps, we turned around barrels and poles and we went over poles on the ground. The obstacles were so easy for me. In the city I had to dodge parking meters and moving cars while loud noises like beeping car horns were going off. Loud noises like car horns usually spooked other horses, but not me. I was used to the loud noises of the city.

Sammy walked me back to the barn and took off my saddle and bridle. She brushed me and walked me around the farm to cool me off.

As we walked together, she told me what she and Fred had talked about. Sammy was going to ride me in the annual Fourth of July Horse and Rider Competition that was to be held in only a few weeks. The competition is the biggest event of the year. The first place prize in the competition is a huge trophy and a big blue ribbon and the horse and rider get to lead the parade at the end of the summer. The parade goes straight down Main Street in town and everyone from the surrounding towns come to see it. Sammy explained that the Worthington's win every year. One year Wendy Worthington won and last year Wallace Worthington won. The Worthington

family is a very wealthy family, and because they have the most expensive horses, they expect to win.

Wendy and Wallace are very mean and nasty to everyone. The Worthington's keep their horses at Fred's farm. They own the beautiful horses that I have been watching everyday since I got to Fred's farm. After listening to Sammy, I realized that I want to win this competition for Sammy and for all the other horses that are not so pretty.

Chapter 4

Sammy and I worked hard every day practicing the obstacles that would be in the race. I was so good at going over the jumps and around all the barrels that Sammy and I were starting to get very excited about the big race. Wendy and Wallace continued to pick on me and Sammy because I wasn't as pretty as their horses, and I was old. Sammy had never competed in any shows or races before. She always dreamed of competing but never had a horse to ride, nor did her family have the money to buy and take care of such a large animal.

Sammy and I moved over every obstacle with record speed, but the only problem was the water obstacle. I had never seen a stream before. In the big city, the only water I saw was mud puddles on the sidewalks. Yesterday, Sammy and I ran all through our obstacle course, and when we got to the stream, I got scared and stopped, and poor Sammy went flying over my head into the water. I felt so bad. Sammy didn't get hurt, but just as that happened, Wendy and Wallace rode by just in time to see the whole thing.

Poor Sammy was sitting in the stream and Wallace yelled, "Just give up Knobby Knees Nolan!" and Wendy yelled, "You don't have a chance of winning with that nag!"

Sammy walked me back to the barn. She was dripping wet from head to toe and she was clearly upset by what the Worthingtons had said. *I have got to get over my fear of water,*

I thought. *How is Sammy supposed to win the big race if I can't even get my feet wet?* The race was only a few weeks away and I felt like I had let Sammy down. Sammy is the only kid at the farm that is nice to me and believes in me. I need to get over my fear of water.

Sammy and I need to win this race and show Wendy and Wallace that we are the best. The Worthington's shouldn't expect to win every year just because they own expensive horses. I'm going to get through the stream, but I just need to figure out how.

Chapter 5

Day in and day out Sammy and I practiced for the big race. We mostly practiced the water obstacle. Each day Sammy and I would try running through the stream and each day Sammy would lead me back to the barn dripping wet from head to toe. I knew I needed to go through the stream, but each time we approached the water, I would get scared and stop, and poor Sammy would end up flying into the water.

There were just a few days left before the big race. I was beside myself with worry about how I was going to go through the stream. Sammy decided to have Fred help get me through the stream. Fred and Sammy led me close to the stream to drink, but I would not go through the stream. I thought I would never get to the other side. I felt like if I went into the water, I would fall into a deep hole. Sammy and Fred tried walking me in, forwards, backward, and sideways, but I was afraid to put my feet in the water. Sammy tried feeding me near the stream to get me used to the water, but I still would not go in. Wendy and Wallace rode right by us and ran through the water telling us to give up. I got so mad at the Worthingtons that I finally put one hoof in the water. The stream was cool and refreshing on this hot day. I put the other hoof in and it wasn't so bad. I didn't like it, but I did it for Sammy and Fred.

Sammy cheered and hugged me. Fred was so relieved he kissed me right on the nose. I hope I can keep my courage up for the big race.

Chapter 6

Race Day finally arrived. It was the Fourth of July, and excitement filled the air. Sammy worked all morning brushing my coat and trimming my mane and tail. I was looking pretty good. Sammy wore a nice pair of boots and a beautiful shirt. Fred bought Sammy a new riding helmet for the race. Fred and Sammy loaded me into a horse trailer to bring me to the race. It was so early in the morning I could hear the birds singing and chirping in the trees.

We arrived at a big park with lots of other horses and riders. The riders were all practicing the obstacles that were set up in preparation for the race.

Fred and Sammy put my saddle on me, and Sammy got in the saddle. We walked and trotted around just to warm up. An announcer called all the horses and riders to the starting gate. We all lined up while a judge told us the rules of the competition. A big checkered flag was lowered to tell us that the race had begun.

Sammy and I rode as fast as we could and went over each jump and around each barrel with record speed. We were ahead of all the other horses and riders. I could see the stream ahead, and I was so scared I ran as fast as I could, but just as I approached the water, I was getting nervous and afraid again.

I stopped right in front of the stream. All the other horses ran past us. Sammy managed to stay on top of me this time. She asked me to make a wide circle, and we approached the stream again. I closed my eyes and ran through the stream as quickly as possible. I was so relieved that the water obstacle was done. The only problem was, we lost time at the stream and now we were in last place. I ran as quickly as I could and started to catch up. Sammy was cheering me on and encouraging me to keep up the quick pace. I could see the finish line and there was no way we could catch up and pass all the other horses and riders. It looked like Wallace and Wendy would come in first and second place. Just as we all finished the last jump, I heard a big bang and saw bright lights. Sammy said the noise and lights were fireworks going off. I wasn't scared. I was used to loud noises from living in the city.

Up ahead, though, all the other horses spooked and threw their riders off.

The horses ran in the opposite direction of the finish line. The noise continued, and Sammy and I rode past all the horses and riders. We could see that Wendy and Wallace were on the ground and their horses were long gone. Sammy and I ran straight through the ribbon marking the finish line. We had done it! We were the first horse-and-rider team that crossed the finish line. It took a while for all the other riders to gather up their horses and continue on to the finish line. None of them were harmed. Wendy and Wallace came in last and second-to-last place.

Chapter 7

Fred came running up to me and Sammy. He hugged Sammy and then he hugged me. He was laughing and grinning from ear to ear. He led us to the winner's circle. Cameras and videos were all around us. Local newspaper reporters were asking dozens of questions. The judge put a wreath of roses that was in the shape of a huge horseshoe around my neck. The judge also handed Sammy a huge trophy and big blue ribbon. Sammy and I were so happy that we won, and I was so happy that I didn't disappoint Sammy.

Sammy smiled at me and said, "Herkimer, good job, boy!" "Now that we won, we have to get ready for our next adventure." "Next month, we're going to swim in the big water competition."

I gulped and felt a wave of anxiety come over me. Sammy laughed and said, " I'm only kidding Herkimer. We have bigger and better adventures, and I promise, they won't involve swimming."

Fred got a bucket of carrots for Herkimer to eat. A man in the crowd walked by eating a jelly donut. Herkimer pulled to go toward the man.

Sammy pulled on the reins to stop Herkimer, and then laughed and said, "No jelly donuts for you Herkimer, just carrots!"

CPSIA information can be obtained
at www.ICGtesting.com
Printed in the USA
LVIW020737090512

280926LV00001B